S0-EIE-345

Illustrations by Carla Cortesi
Ideation by Maria Luisa Benigni

Original Title: *Baby Gesù*
© 1991 Figlie di San Paolo, via Albani, 21 — 20149 Milano

Translated by Mary David Wickenhiser, fsp

ISBN 0-8198-6972-4
English edition © 1994, Daughters of St. Paul

Printed and published in the U.S.A. by St. Paul Books & Media, 50 St. Paul's Ave., Boston, MA 02130

St. Paul Books & Media is the publishing house of the Daughters of St. Paul, an international congregation of women religious serving the Church with the communications media.

1 2 3 4 5 6 7 8 9   99 98 97 96 95 94

The Story of
Baby Jesus

by Marina Luzi

Pauline

ST. PAUL BOOKS & MEDIA

Many, many years ago,
almost two thousand years ago,
in a small town in Palestine,
something very special happened.
When you get a little older you will be able to read
about this special event in the Gospels.

The town was Nazareth.
The young girl was Mary
and her parents were
Ann and Joachim.

Mary was engaged
to a young man named Joseph.

One day, Mary was doing the things she did every day, praying and working. All of a sudden, the room was filled with a bright light. And a voice said to her, "Good morning, Mary!"

Mary was very surprised and almost frightened.
But the voice told her, "Don't be afraid, Mary.
I am the angel Gabriel. I have good news for you.
It will make you very happy."

" I come in God's name.
God loves you very much.
He wants you to be
the mother of His Son.
The baby will be called
Jesus and he will save
his people."

With that special light all around her, and the voice of the angel to give her courage, Mary was happy to say yes. Then, she thought about Joseph. She asked the angel to explain how this could happen.

Hurray!

Praise the Lord! I will be the mother of Jesus.

The angel understood Mary's question,
and went to tell the good news
to Joseph.

Joseph had worked
hard all day.
He was tired and
had fallen asleep right
on top of his work table.
The angel's voice
woke him up.

Don't be afraid of anything.
Get married just like you planned to do.
Love Mary and love the baby who will be born.

Joseph
felt like the happiest
man in the world.
He knew that
he had been chosen
to love and take of
God's Son.

I'm so happy!

After the visit of the angel,
Mary and Joseph
got married.
The celebration lasted
a few days because that's
what the people at that
time used to do.

The days went by peacefully in the house
of Joseph and Mary. Joseph prepared the wood
to make a little crib. Mary made little clothes for
the baby soon to be born.

Finally, everything was ready: the crib and the toys, the clothes and a blanket made by Mary.

One day some news was given
that upset the people in the town.
The Roman Emperor wanted to know how many
people there were in his empire, so, he gave an order
that everybody had to return to the town where they
were born and sign their names in a big book.

We have to go, too.

Joseph was born in Bethlehem. Nazareth and Bethlehem were far apart and at that time there were no cars, or trains, or airplanes.

Joseph was worried about Mary. And Mary was worried about the baby soon to be born.

Early one morning, Joseph loaded the donkey with the things they would need for the trip. He also took a bag filled with all the things for the new baby. Then they left for Bethlehem.

The donkey was tired and cold, and out of breath. Mary was sitting on the donkey but she never complained. She only thought about the tiny baby she was carrying inside of her.

The trip was long and tiresome.
Some days it rained. Other days the sun came out.
And sometimes cold and icy winds blew.

Lake of Tiberias

Nazareth

Mediterranean Sea

Nights turned into days, and days turned into nights.
Mary and Joseph crossed over flat ground and hills.
They traveled through villages and towns.
Finally, they arrived in Bethlehem.

Jordan River

Dead Sea

Jerusalem

Bethlehem

The streets in Bethlehem
were full of people.
All of the hotels were
already full, too.

Joseph just wanted a quiet place
where Mary could rest,
but it was very hard to find one.

Joseph knocked on door after door,
but every place was full.
There was no room for
Mary and Joseph to stay.

It was already dark and no one would open their door
to Mary and Joseph. Mary was tired and cold,
and the donkey was getting upset.

Finally, someone felt sorry
for Joseph and Mary.
He showed them
some caves
on the side of the hills,
not far from Bethlehem.

Joseph thanked him and looked for an empty cave.
When he found one, he took some dry straw
and made a bed for Mary.

There was a cow in the cave but Joseph wasn't worried. He tied the donkey to the manger, then he covered Mary with his coat so that she would be warm.

Joseph did not sleep.
He watched the shepherds out on the hillside
and stayed awake in case Mary needed anything.

Then, in the middle o the night,
as the stars twinkled
in the dark blue sky,
Baby Jesus was born.
Joseph heard the baby cry
but he knew everything was all
right because Mary was
smiling and happy.

Joseph put his arms around Mary and the new born Baby Jesus. He wanted to show Mary and Jesus that he would always love and take care of them.
Then, Joseph and Mary said a prayer to thank God.

It was very cold in the cave and the little Baby cried.
Joseph laid him in the manger near the cow
and the donkey so that their breath could keep
Baby Jesus warm.

Mary did not talk very much. She was praying.
In her heart she sang
the most beautiful lullaby in the world.

There were some shepherds with their sheep camped
near the cave. An angel called them.
"Quick, wake up.
The Savior you have waited so long for has been born."

"Go. You will find him wrapped
in swaddling clothes and lying in a manger."

The shepherds took their sheep and ran to the cave to see the new born Savior. And the angels continued to sing, "Glory to God in highest heaven and peace on earth to the people God loves."

That same night, three wise men from the East
saw a great big star.
It was a comet with a beautiful, bright tail.

The three wise men understood right away that
something very special had happened.
They got their camels ready and started out on their
journey to find the newborn Savior.

Their names were Gaspar, Melchior and Balthasar.
They followed the special star that looked like it was
moving through the other stars in the sky.

49

They followed the star day and night, night and day.
When they reached Bethlehem, the star stopped over
the cave and shone even brighter.
The wise men understood what this meant
so they stopped their caravan.

They entered the cave and
because they knew that the baby
in Mary's arms was the Savior,
they all knelt down. The three magi gave
Baby Jesus gifts of gold, frankincense and myrrh.
The news about the arrival of three kings spread
throughout the whole area.

Everyone was filled with joy because the Savior had finally come to live among the people.

Ever since that very first
Christmas, every year Christians
all over the world remember
the birth of Jesus.
Each country has its own way
to celebrate this great day
and to thank God
for sending His Son.

December
25
Jesus' Birthday

Christians in every corner of the world, from every country, remember and celebrate the birth of Jesus.

Bells ring, bagpipes play, candles are lighted,
and everyone, from the biggest to the smallest,
sings Christmas carols.

Family and friends exchange gifts and greetings.
Relatives and friends visit one another.
Some people prepare a table of food
for the poor or the homeless
who do not have family or friends.

Christmas is a big holiday because that's the day we
celebrate the birth of Jesus.
Because Jesus is everyone's brother,
that makes us all brothers and sisters.
We are all children of the same Father in heaven.